The Untold Story
of
Falling Stars

™

Written and Illustrated
by
Wayne Smith

This book belongs to:

_____

"Every child, both young and the young at heart has seen and wished upon a falling star. This delightful story stirs the imagination in the child in all of us. I am touched by it's creativity and energy. Just keep reaching for those stars."

Estelle Getty
Sophia on "The Golden Girls".

A legend is a tale fondly remembered throughout the years. This particular story happens to be a secret, one that has been kept that way for a very long time. Have you ever looked up into the sky at night and wondered what happens to falling stars?

At last, the answer to that age old
question can finally be revealed.
The magical world of Starbabies is
something most children have never heard
of, or even dreamed about;
that is, until tonight........

long time ago, there was a land far away. In this land were many strange and wonderful things. There were purple valleys, blue trees, and bright green lakes with Epazoodles. You've never heard of an Epazoodle? I'll tell you about those later. There was even a place known as Upside Down Canyon, where everything was, you guessed it, upside down. There were rivers and oceans made of chocolate syrup.

This land was quite different than anything you have ever seen, but the most amazing thing about it was the sky. It was filled with stars, more than you could ever imagine. One night, stars began to fall from the sky and every time one landed in this unknown place, it came to life. After arriving in this enchanted land the stars became known as Starbabies.

It was a cold, dark night in this land far
away, when suddenly a bright golden light fell
from the sky. It was a falling star.

Slowly, he opened his eyes, because he never had eyes before, and what he saw was beautiful. The little star was thrilled to be there, but quickly noticed he was the only star around. And so he named himself First Star. Morning came and First Star became very sleepy. Stars usually sleep during the daytime, so they can light up the sky at night.

He quickly found a blue tree, climbed into it and fell asleep, dreaming of living in this new enchanted land. When he woke, First Star built a home in the big blue tree. He made a bedroom, a living room and a small dining room.

    When his work was done, he went exploring. While walking
along, he thought to himself, "It sure would be nice to have a
friend." It was true, he had no one to talk to or play with.
And so he went to sleep in his new bed, in his new home, a
very lonely First Star.

When night came, First Star heard a strange noise. He ran outside and listened real hard. It sounded like a low growl and seemed to be coming from Upside Down Canyon. Too scared to investigate, he went back inside to the safety of his tree house.

When the noise stopped, First Star went outside to play. It was then he saw a strange glow coming from the sky. It seemed to be leading to Upside Down Canyon. Upside Down Canyon was a funny place, as soon as you crossed its border, everything was upside down,

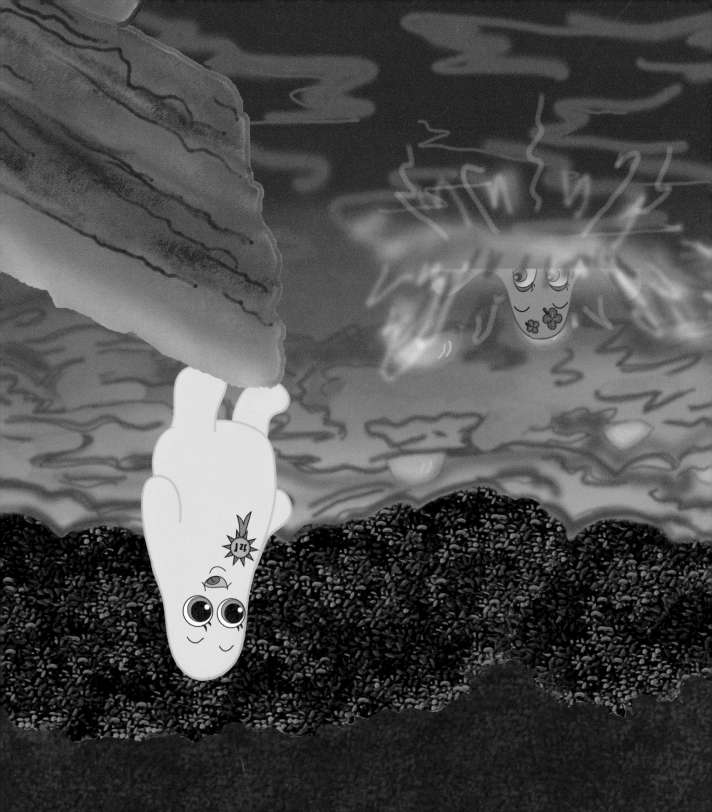

including you! He decided to find out what all the
commotion was. As he got to the canyon, he saw something
splashing around in a green lake. It looked like another star.
Oh, he hoped it was!

First Star dove into the water and started swimming out to where the little star was, when all at once, from the depths of the green lake, came a dreadful Epazoodle. Remember earlier I told you I'd tell you about Epazoodles? Well, they are mean ugly creatures with scales and horns and live at the bottom of the green lake. They eat anything that comes into the water, including Starbabies. The Epazoodle decided to make the new star his dinner.

15

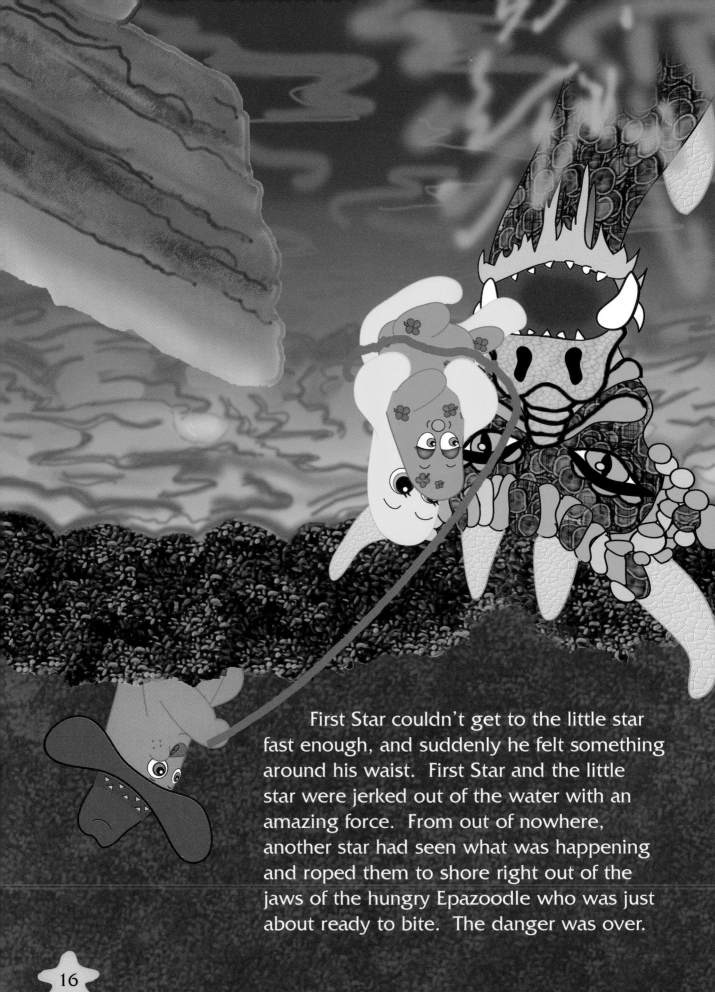

First Star couldn't get to the little star fast enough, and suddenly he felt something around his waist. First Star and the little star were jerked out of the water with an amazing force. From out of nowhere, another star had seen what was happening and roped them to shore right out of the jaws of the hungry Epazoodle who was just about ready to bite. The danger was over.

As the three stars sat on the bank of the green lake, they knew they needed to stick together. So they promised to remain friends forever. First Star decided to name his new found friends, since after all, he was first. The star who had saved them all would be know as Lone Star, because he alone came to their rescue. The little star was named Lucky Star, because he was quite lucky to be there at all. First Star looked at his two new friends and said, "I'm happy now that I have friends, from now on, we aren't just stars, we are Starbabies."

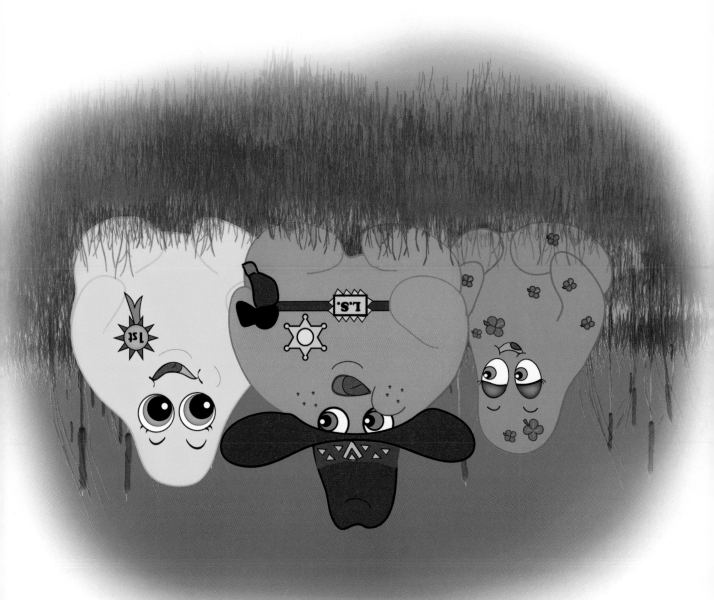

17

Nights passed and the little trio became best buddies. They did many favors for one another. They helped with daily chores and even managed to play a little bit: well maybe a lot.

Each star truly lived up to his new name. Lone Star proved his bravery by always helping with the scariest of situations. Lucky Star was always just that, lucky. First Star, who would always be first, seemed to always have the best ideas. "Let's go to the Purple Valley! Maybe there we'll find out why we are here, and not up in the sky like all the other stars." The others agreed and they left on their long journey.

It took two nights to reach the Purple Valley. On the way, they had to pass through Food Forest. Food Forest was a place where everything was made out of food. There were hot dog bushes, french fry plants, cotton candy trees, and even chocolate chip mushrooms. The Starbabies spent the day sleeping inside a popcorn tree.

When they woke, Lucky Star noticed most of the popcorn was missing. Many of the chocolate chip mushrooms were also missing. They heard someone moaning on the other side of the tree.

21

     As the Starbabies raced to see where the sounds were
coming from, they saw a rather plump blue star lying on his back
with his arms folded over his tummy. "Oh, I feel so bad," said the
new star. First Star held out his hand and said, "My friend, you
will feel better soon, you just ate too much food. From now on,
you will be called Hungry Star." Hungry Star slowly stood up and
joined the group, who continued their trip to Purple Valley.

Morning came, and the stars reached their destination. Purple Valley was more beautiful than they had imagined. It seemed like everything was a different shade of purple. Hungry Star saw some berries on a bush and quickly began to eat them. First Star, who had already started to look around, shouted, "Hey, look! A trail; let's follow it and see where it leads." The Starbabies began to run down the purple trail. hoping to find excitement.

Suddenly, the valley grew strangely quiet and the stars got scared, all except Lone Star, who said, "It feels like someone is staring at us." It was true, they all felt as though someone was watching them through the bushes.

All at once, hundreds of tiny purple creatures came out of the woods. Each one was oddly different, some covered in purple hair, some had purple feathers, and some even had wings.

Just then, the creature with the largest wings said, "I am Plima, King of the Poolies. We welcome you to Poolie Town." The Starbabies were glad the Poolies were friendly and accepted their hospitality.

That night, the Poolies gave a party in honor of the
Starbabies, it was a fabulous feast with all kinds of food and fun.

Some of the Poolies even put together a little show to entertain the Starbabies.   King Plima asked the Starbabies to stay in Poolie Town and become honorary Poolies. The stars were flattered, but since they couldn't find an answer as to why they were here in this land, they had to keep looking. King Plima understood, and told them they were welcome anytime.

He handed First Star a magic purple Poolie feather. "With this feather, you will have good luck. Anytime you need help, point the feather toward the Purple Valley and you will get the help you need." King Plima also warned, "Be wise, you can only use the feather once, that's all the magic it has." First Star took the feather and all the stars thanked King Plima and went on their way.

The Starbabies had gone a few miles when Lone Star said, "Let's take a different road home, maybe it will lead us to the answer to our question." Instead of going the way they had come, they went over a rock and through a field, hoping to find a clue why they were in this fascinating land.

Soon, the sky got very dark and the wind began to blow. The little stars became frightened. One of the dark clouds began to get closer and closer until it almost touched the ground. Just then, another dark cloud came down on the other side of the stars. Now the little stars were really scared, all except Lone Star, who said. "There's nothing to be afraid of."

Suddenly, they heard a terrible laugh, "Ha, ha, ha, ha, ha, I am Vivica, the wicked dark cloud. I am here to take you to a place where it always rains and you can never go out and play!"

The Starbabies felt all was lost, until First Star remembered the magic purple Poolie feather. He quickly pointed it toward Purple Valley and wished for Vivica to disappear. Evil Vivica shouted, "You tricked me, I thought this would be easy. I'll be back when you least expect me."

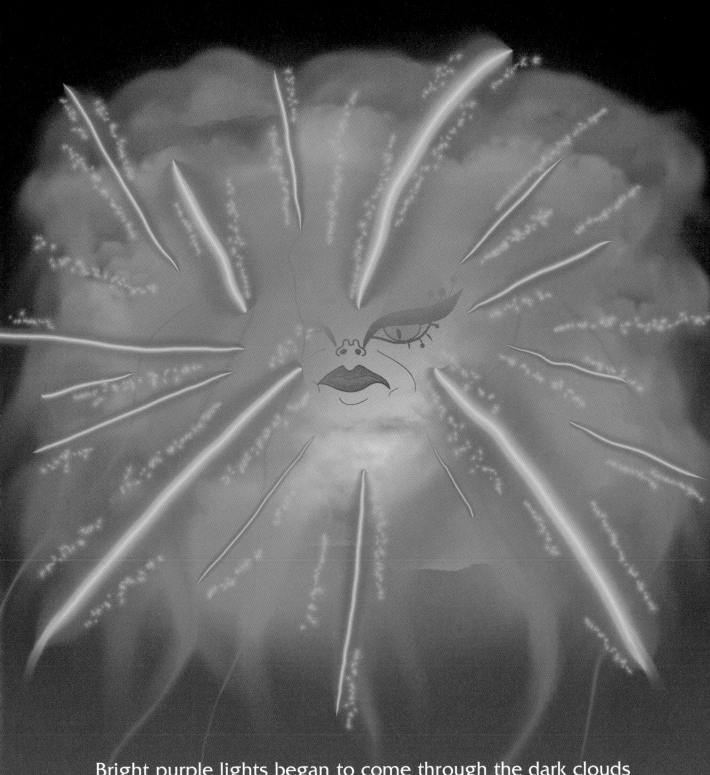

Bright purple lights began to come through the dark clouds until Vivica was gone, and so was the lucky feather's magic. The Starbabies were relieved, and hurried back to the main road, running all the way home.

The Starbabies were pleased when they got home. They were also surprised when they saw three new stars waiting for them. First Star noticed right away a funny star who had a slanted mouth and curvy arms. "Your name is now Crooked Star," said First Star to the comical little star. Crooked Star smiled and said, "Thank you, I've always wanted a name."

Then a white star with pretty red trim came over and hugged First Star. "We're so happy to be here, I love you all," she said. First Star blushed and said, "I think I'll name you Love Star because you seem to be so full of love."

Then First Star noticed the last of the three new stars crying. He walked over and put his arms around her. The crying star said, "I don't know why I'm crying, it's just so touching."

First Star decided to name her Sad Star because she seemed so sad. The new stars were glad to be there with their new friends but began to wonder why they weren't up in the sky like the other stars. "I would love to know why we are all here," said Love Star. Somehow none of the Starbabies could find a good answer.

Days and nights went by and the little stars grew very close. Still, they couldn't help but wonder what brought them to this far away land. They held meetings, explored the land and still found no clues.

Then one night they saw a beam of light coming down the road. It grew brighter and brighter, until suddenly, they saw two new stars approaching the tree houses. Lone Star and First Star raced to greet them.

"Welcome little stars," said First Star. One of the new stars played a bright red guitar and sang a funny little song. First Star was so impressed he named him Rock Star, because he was so talented. The next star was easy to name because she was so glamorous. The bright pink star with all the diamonds would be called Movie Star.

New stars always got a birthday party when they arrived, so Rock Star and Movie Star were no different. The party was almost over when First Star shouted loudly, "I've got it, I've got it, the reason we are all here in this land."

All the other Starbabies gathered around First Star with anticipation as he said, "Fellow stars, we have all looked for an answer when the answer was here all the time. We are here in this land to be together, and help one another. We are here to be a family and live in our new city, Starrywood." Everyone cheered as First Star gave them the answer, and a name for their new city.

STARRYWOOD

Starrywood grew each time a new falling star would arrive, and before long, it was quite a large city. Through it all, the Starbabies remained as happy and lovable as they had always been. Because, after all, they had the one thing that made them so happy, a family.

42

So, if some night, you should
happen to look up in the sky and
see a falling star, remember, he's
just going to join the others in that
fabulous land of the little lost
Starbabies.

43

I would like to dedicate "Starbabies the
Untold Story of Falling Stars" to my family
for all their love and support. To my mother
for her patience and love. To my brother for
being my rock. To my sister for being a child
along with me. To my father who would
have been proud. And last but definitly not
least, my grandmother, Mattie, for reading
those old stories to me.

Wayne Smith

™

uncle wayne's toy company, inc.

Waxahachie, Texas